Dealing with Feelings:

I'm Scared

Written by Elizabeth Crary
Illustrated by Jean Whitney

Why a Book on Fear?

Parents often ask me for help dealing with their children's feelings. This may be because many people were taught to ignore their feelings as children. Now they want to raise their own children differently, but have no idea how.

How can this book help?

I'm Scared can help children accept their feelings and decide how to respond.

The book models a constructive process for handling fear. It shows a parent and child discussing feelings openly. The story also offers specific options for children. There are verbal, physical, and creative ways described to express feelings. In addition, *I'm Scared* serves as a role model for parents who wish to change the way they respond to their children's feelings.

How to use *I'm Scared*

I'm Scared becomes more useful with time and repetition. A couple of readings probably won't make a dramatic change. But you can start to help your child transfer the information to real life.

Distinguish between feelings and actions. Read the book, letting the child choose the options. Ask, "How does Tracy *feel* now? What will she *do* next?" at the end of each page.

Introduce different options. Children need several ways to cope with feelings that work for them. This story offers ten ideas. When you are done reading, ask your child, "What else could Tracy have done?" Record your child's responses on the "Idea Page" at the end.

Use as a springboard for discussing other situations. Begin by discussing something that happened to someone else. Ask your child to identify the feelings and the alternatives the child tried. Talk with your child from the perspective of collecting information, rather than what is right or wrong.

For example, assume a visiting friend, Mike, did not want to go home. Ask, "How did Mike *feel* when it was time to go home?" "What did he do first when he felt upset?" "What else did he do?" Possible answers might be: he ignored the request, he said "No", or he scowled and said "Okay."

When your child can distinguish between feelings and behavior for other people, you can review something he did in the same nonjudgmental way.

Elizabeth Crary, Seattle, Washington

Copyright © 1994 by Elizabeth Crary
Illustrations by Jean Whitney

ISBN 0-943990-89-0 Paper
ISBN 0-943990-90-4 Library binding
LC 93-085377

Parenting Press, Inc.
P.O. Box 75267
Seattle, WA 98125

Feelings and the Parent's Role

One of your jobs as a parent or teacher is to help children understand and deal with their feelings. Children need basic information about feelings, they need to have their feelings validated, and they need to have tools to deal with those feelings. These are discussed below.

1. Develop a vocabulary.
Children may feel overwhelmed by intense feelings. One simple way to begin understanding feelings is to label them.

■ Share your feelings: "I feel frustrated when I spill coffee on the floor."

■ Read books that discuss feelings, like the *Let's Talk About Feelings* series.

■ Observe another's feelings: "I'll bet he's proud of that A+ grade."

In addition, introduce your child to different words for related feelings—for example, mad, furious, angry, upset, etc.

2. Help children distinguish between feelings and actions.
Understand that feelings are neither good nor bad. Feeling mad is neither good nor bad. However, hitting is a behavior. Hitting is not acceptable. You can say, "It's okay to be mad, but I cannot let you hit your sister."

3. Validate the child's feelings.
Many people have been trained to ignore or suppress their feelings. Girls are often taught that being mad is unfeminine or not nice. Boys are taught not to cry. You can validate children's feelings by listening to them and reflecting the feeling. Listen without judging. Remain separate.

Remember, your child's feelings belong to her/him.

When you reflect the feeling ("You are mad that Stephanie has to go home now"), you are not attempting to solve the problem. Reflecting, or acknowledging the feeling helps the child deal with it.

4. Offer children several ways to cope with their feelings.
If telling children to "Use your words" worked for most kids, grown-ups would have little trouble with children's feelings. Children need a variety of ways to respond—auditory, physical, visual, creative, and self-nurturing. Once a child has experienced a variety of responses, you can ask what he or she would like to try.

For example: "Do you want to feel mad right now or do you want to change your feeling?" If your child wants to change, you could say, "What could you do? Let's see, you could run around the block, make a card to send to Stephanie, talk about the feeling, or read your favorite book." After you've generated ideas, let the child choose what works for her. Often all children need is to have their feelings acknowledged.

Be gentle with yourself.
Remember, some situations are resolved quickly and others take time and repetition. Hold a vision of what you would like for your child and yourself, and acknowledge the progress you have made.

Tracy could hardly wait. Today she would meet her new neighbors. She saw three kids' bikes, so there must be three in the family. She hoped there would be someone her age. Her best friend had moved away and she still felt lonely.

"Momma, do you think they have someone my age?" she asked as she and her brother helped her mom make cookies. "One of the bikes is about my size."

"It's possible," Mom replied.

"Do you really think so?" Tracy asked.

"You will have to wait and find out," Mom said.

"But I want to know now!" Tracy moaned. "Oh well, I'll pretend I have a new friend. She will like baseball, and riding bikes, and reading. And she'll hate dogs—especially big dogs—just like me. Her favorite color will be blue, and. . . ."

"Tracy," her brother called from the living room, "there's a car pulling in the driveway next door." Before he finished the sentence, Tracy's nose was pressed against the window.

"I can't see," she wailed. "The kids are all getting out of the other side." She raced to the kitchen to ask, "Mom, how long do I have to wait before I can take the cookies we baked over?"

"Not long," Paul called, as the doorbell rang.

Tracy started to follow Paul outside, but suddenly her smile vanished from her face. On the steps stood three kids and a dog! **A big, bouncy dog.** Tracy was terrified.

What do you think Tracy can do?

Listen to any ideas your child has. If he or she has no ideas, turn the page.

"Mom," Tracy cried, as she ran back to the kitchen. "There is a dog outside. I'm scared! He might bite like Rover did."

"Some dogs can hurt. And some can be lots of fun. Feeling scared is a clue you may be in danger. When you feel scared check and see if you are safe, then decide what to do. Does this dog look dangerous?" Mom asked.

"No," Tracy answered, "but I don't know what to do."

"Well, I can think of several things you can do," Mom replied calmly. "You could—

Watch from inside . . . . page 10
Ask the kids to take the dog home . . . . page 12
Ask someone to hold your hand
        and meet the kids . . . . page 14
Take five deep breaths . . . . page 18
Sing a happy song . . . . page 20

Is that enough ideas to start with?"

Tracy nodded.

What will you try first?" her mother asked.

Which do you think Tracy will try first?

Turn to the page your child chooses. If no idea is chosen, turn the page.

Watch from Inside

"I'm too scared to go out. I'll watch from the living room," Tracy decided.

She walked slowly to the window and looked out. The new kids were all laughing at something her brother said. "I wish I knew what they were talking about," she thought.

As the kids talked, she watched the dog rush up to Paul and sniff him. Then the dog bounced around and jumped up on him. Paul laughed and pushed him down. "It's funny," Tracy thought, "when I'm inside the dog doesn't look so scary."

Paul saw her watching out the window and brought the neighbors over. "Come on out, Tracy. Frisky is very friendly. He won't hurt you. He's on a leash."

Just then Frisky jumped up on Paul and almost knocked him down. Tracy's heart started to race and she could hardly breathe. "No, thank you," she replied. "I don't feel like it now." She wanted to join them, but she was very scared.

What do you think Tracy will do?

Ask the kids to take the dog home   page 12
Take Mom's hand and go out   . . . page 14

Ask the Kids to Take the Dog Home

Tracy thought for a few minutes, then she called to the children, "Could you take your dog home and come back?"

"Not now," the older boy replied. "Frisky's been cooped up in the car all day. We're supposed to let him run around. Why don't you come out and meet him? He's really very friendly."

"I don't like dogs much. He's so big and so bouncy I'm scared of him," she admitted.

"I used to be scared of dogs, too. But now Frisky is my good friend. I'll run him around the block until he slows down. Then I'll show you how to make friends with him."

Ask Someone to Hold Hands

Tracy really wanted to meet the new girl, but she was so, so afraid of their dog.

When the kids got back from walking the dog, Tracy took her mom's hand and went out to meet them. She was shaking in her sandals, but felt a little better holding someone's hand.

Paul introduced the neighbors, "Tracy, this is Matt and Gabrielle, and their stepbrother, Jonathan, with Frisky. Neighbors, this is my sister Tracy and my mom."

"Hi," Tracy said, as she clung to her mother's hand. While she talked to Gabrielle, Tracy watched Frisky sniff around. Even though he was wandering a bit, she could see Jonathan was holding the leash tightly. Slowly, Tracy let go of her mother's hand and the girls sat on the front steps to talk.

"Uh oh. We have to go home soon," Gabrielle said when she noticed the time. "Would you like to make friends with Frisky before we go?"

"I guess," Tracy said. She could feel the fear start to come back just thinking about getting closer to Frisky.

Turn to page 16.

Make Friends with the Dog

Tracy talked herself into making friends with the dog. "After all," she told herself, "Paul won't let Frisky hurt me."

The older boy gave his brother the leash and knelt to her level. "My name is Jonathan. Frisky has never bitten anyone, but he is curious. He's as curious about you, as you are scared of him. See how he is pulling the leash so he can meet you?"

She nodded, saying, "I'm glad he's curious, not hungry."

"To make friends with a dog," Jonathan said, "you hold your hand out like this and let the dog come and sniff you. Frisky might jump on you. He might even lick you, but he won't bite you. Now, stretch your hand out like me."

Tracy held out her hand timidly. Frisky moved forward to sniff. As he came closer she repeated to herself, "They won't let him hurt me. They won't let him hurt me." When he touched her hand she started to jerk away, but stopped herself. "Well," she thought, "I'm still scared, but not as much as before."

What do you think Tracy will do?

Take a deep breath and pet Frisky   page 18
Ask how others stop being afraid   page 22

Take Five Deep Breaths

"I'd like to pet the dog, but I'm too scared," Tracy repeated.

"Sometimes when I'm scared," her brother Paul said, "I stop breathing. When I don't breathe right, all I can think of is being scared. But when I take five deep breaths I feel better. You could take a couple of breaths and then pet Frisky."

"Okay, I'll try," she said, but the thought frightened her even more. She stood there a moment, paralyzed. Suddenly, she noticed she wasn't breathing. Maybe her brother was right, she thought, and took a deep breath in and let it out slowly.

"This is better," she said and took another breath. The air seemed to calm the scared feelings. She took another breath and slowly reached out towards the dog. Frisky turned to face her and she could feel the panic start again. She moved away and then noticed she wasn't breathing anymore.

She took another breath and then tentatively touched Frisky's head. Slowly she moved her hand down his neck. "The fur is smooth and sort of stiff," she remarked to herself.

Tracy felt better. "I'm still scared," she told Paul, "but it is not so bad if I remember to just keep breathing."

Turn to page 20.

Sing a Happy Song

The next day Tracy wanted to visit her new friend Gabrielle. "I don't know what to do," Tracy moaned to herself. "I want to play with Gabrielle, but I'm scared of Frisky. He is sure to bark and jump on me. What can I do?"

"I know!" she exclaimed. "I can sing Granddad's song —

Stand up tall, don't feel small.
Sing a song of cheer
To chase away your fear.

Tracy crept next door. When she opened the neighbor's gate, she could hear Frisky begin to bark inside the house. She took a deep breath and started to sing to herself.

The singing took her mind off the barking. She knocked on the door. "Can Gabrielle come out and play?" she asked.

"Sure," said Gabrielle's mother. "Do you want to come inside while I get her?" she asked.

"No, thanks," Tracy replied. "I'll wait outside."

What do you think Tracy will do?

Ask others how to stop being afraid page 22
Make a plan . . . . page 24